Fishing with
Grandma

Fishing with Grandma

by Susan Avingaq and Maren Vsetula

Illustrated by Charlene Chua

As Jeela and I ran up to *Anaanatsiaq*'s house, we could see her through the frosty window, sitting on the floor with a large sealskin in her lap.

My sister and I were excited for a visit with our favourite elder, and we were hoping to convince her to take us out for an adventure!

"Hello, kids! It's so nice to see you!" Grandma said as we ran through the door.

"Hi, Anaanatsiaq!" we said.

The house smelled of fresh bannock and we could hear upbeat fiddle music playing on the radio.

3

Once inside, I grabbed some string that was lying on the coffee table, and Jeela and I played string games as Grandma sewed.

"Anaanatsiaq," I said, after a few minutes, "we would love to go on an adventure with you today."

"That sounds like fun," Grandma replied. "What were you thinking?"

I saw that Jeela had made a fish with her string. "How about jigging for fish?" I suggested.

"*Atii*, let's go!" Grandma cried. She was always happy to get outside and show us new things.

Grandma told us what clothing and equipment we needed to bring in order to stay warm.

She told me to layer my clothing so that I would not sweat when I chipped the ice.

In the fall, when the ice is just starting to form, it is thin and perfect for jigging.

Jeela and I ran home and picked up all the clothes we would need for the day.

"A trip to the lake! Aren't you kids lucky!" Mom exclaimed.

Grandma prepared snacks and a thermos, and we worked together to get all the equipment from the shed and loaded onto the ATV. We put on our helmets and set off.

It was a crisp, sunny October day and I was glad Grandma had told us to bundle up!

There was already some snow on the ground, enough for people to harness their sled dogs. In the distance, we could see some *inuksuit* on the hills north of the community.

We held on tight as we drove down the bumpy road,
rounding many turns, toward the frozen lake.

As we approached the ice, I could see it was very smooth and flat. There were already people jigging all across the lake.

Grandma parked the ATV on the shoreline and Jeela hopped off and excitedly ran around in the snow.

Grandma explained how to test the ice to make sure it was safe to walk on. She jabbed a long rod into the ice to see if it would break through. If the rod did not break the ice, it was safe to walk on.

We then took our gear out onto the smooth, glassy surface.

"This will be a good spot," Grandma told us, "not too deep and not too shallow."

I was pretty sure my anaanatsiaq knew everything!

"This is a *tuuq*," Grandma explained, holding up a long wooden tool with a sharp chisel blade at the end.

"It is used to make a hole in the ice. Lift it up and thrust it into the ice, slowly chipping away the ice to make a hole."

Grandma demonstrated a few times before handing the tuuq to me.

I happily grabbed hold and began chipping.

"Wow, this is hard work!" I said.

As I continued to work, Grandma scooped away the ice chips from the hole using an ice skimmer.

After a few more minutes, water suddenly came rushing up through the ice.

"*Alianait!*" Grandma exclaimed. "One hole done, two more to go!"

When the holes were finished, Grandma showed us how to prepare our fishing lines to jig.

"The fish like flashy colours," said Grandma, "so we should always use brightly coloured lures. My favourites are lures with red on them. The fish really like those!"

I decided to try a brilliant pink lure.

"Uncoil your line into the hole," Grandma told us, "until it is just above the lake bottom, about ten feet down."

We followed Grandma's instructions, lowering our lines into the water. We were finally ready to start jigging.

"Just hold your jigging sticks and make small movements with your wrists," Grandma shouted from her hole.

"Wow, I can see the bottom of the lake. I can even see some fish swimming by!" I yelled back.

From time to time, I would look up from my fishing hole and listen to the sounds of the lake. Ravens flew by, calling "kak kak." I could also hear Skidoos and ATVs in the distance. Every now and then, I heard excited voices shouting, "It's going to your hole!" or "I got it!"

The ice was alive with wonderful sounds.

After lying at my hole for a while, focusing on my line, I suddenly felt a small bite. "A fish, I've got a fish!" I yelled.

"Alianait!" Grandma called back excitedly. "Pull up the line as fast as you can so that you hook it!"

Grandma came over to my hole and showed me how to bop the fish on the head to stop it from squirming. Jeela eagerly watched.

We continued to jig for the rest of the day, only taking a break to have tea and some yummy bannock.

We ended up catching a lot of Arctic char, far too many for our family to eat.

"What will we do with our catch, Anaanatsiaq?" Jeela asked.

"There are many people who are not able to come out to the lakes. We will deliver fish to them," she replied. "It is always important to think of others."

At the end of the day, when we were back in town, we made deliveries, stopping at the homes of many elders to share our fish.

When we got back to Grandma's house, she fried up the remaining fish and we had a delicious dinner with our parents. I felt so proud and also very tired from our great adventure with Grandma.

Before we went home, Grandma gave us each a big hug.

"It is important to learn traditional skills and to know how to be prepared. Knowing what to bring, where to go, and what to do will help you to always have successful trips," she said with a smile.

I gave her a big squeeze and said, "Thank you for teaching us. I can't wait for our next adventure!"

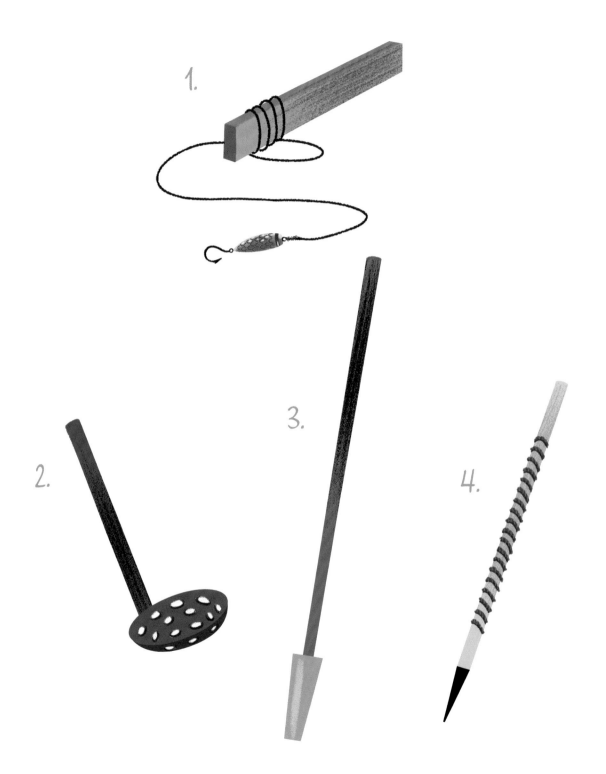

1.

2.

3.

4.

Inuit Fishing Tools

1. Fishing line and jigging stick: A very simple fishing rod made out of wood and fishing line. Sometimes recycled hockey sticks are used as jigging sticks.

2. Ice skimmer: A hand tool used to scoop floating ice chips out of a fishing hole.

3. Tuuq (pronounced "took"): A chisel used to break through ice.

4. Ice probe: A metal rod used to check the thickness of thin ice.

Inuktitut Terms

Alianait (pronounced "a-lee-a-night"): An Inuktitut term used when someone is excited to celebrate.

Anaanatsiaq (pronounced "a-na-nat-see-ak"): The Inuktitut term for "grandmother."

Atii (pronounced "a-tee"): An Inuktitut word meaning "to go" or "let's go."

Inuksuit (pronounced "in-uk-su-eet"): The Inuktitut word for traditional Inuit stone markers.

Contributors

Susan Avingaq was born on the land and moved to the community of Igloolik, Nunavut, in the mid-1970s. She loves to go camping and fishing whenever she can and often brings new people along to teach them these land skills. She enjoys sewing and teaching younger people important cultural practices. She is an extremely resourceful person and thinks that this is an important quality to pass on to the younger generation. She has many grandchildren, with whom she likes to share her stories.

Maren Vsetula is a teacher and educational writer for Inhabit Media. She loves to spend as much time on the land as she can, hiking, fishing, paddling, and dogsledding. She has lived and worked in Nunavut for over a decade.

Charlene Chua worked as a web designer, senior graphic designer, web producer, and interactive project manager before she decided to pursue illustration as a career. Her work has appeared in *American Illustration*, *Spectrum*, and SILA's *Illustration West*, as well as several art books. She illustrated the children's picture books *Julie Black Belt: The Kung Fu Chronicles* and *Julie Black Belt: The Belt of Fire*. She lives in Toronto.

I dedicate this book to my youngest daughter, Elisapee Avingaq.

—SA

This book is dedicated to all adults who make an effort to get kids outside.

—MV

Published by Inhabit Media Inc. • www.inhabitmedia.com
Inhabit Media Inc. (Iqaluit) P.O. Box 11125, Iqaluit, Nunavut, X0A 1H0 • (Toronto) 146A Orchard
View Blvd., Toronto, Ontario, M4R 1C3

Design and layout copyright © 2015 Inhabit Media Inc.
Text copyright © 2015 Susan Avingaq and Maren Vsetula
Illustrations by Charlene Chua © 2015 Inhabit Media Inc.
Photograph (page 29) © Larissa MacDonald

Editors: Louise Flaherty, Neil Christopher
Art director: Danny Christopher

We acknowledge the support of the Canada Council for the Arts for our publishing program.

We acknowledge the support of the Government of Canada through the Department of Canadian
Heritage Canada Book Fund program.

ISBN: 978-1-77227-084-6

Printed in Canada

Library and Archives Canada Cataloguing in Publication

 Vsetula, Maren, 1979-, author
      Fishing with grandma / by Maren Vsetula and Susan Avingaq
; illustrated by Charlene Chua.

ISBN 978-1-77227-084-6 (paperback)

     1. Ice fishing--Juvenile fiction. 2. Grandmothers--Juvenile fiction.
3. Grandchildren--Juvenile fiction. I. Avingaq, Susan, author II. Chua,
Charlene, 1980-, illustrator III. Title.

PS8643.S78F58 2016   jC813'.6   C2016-900768-5